D1137204

C016153672

First published in 1995 by Scholastic Children's Books
This edition first published in 2011 by Scholastic Children's Books
This edition first published in paperback in 2013 by Scholastic Children's Books
Euston House, 24 Eversholt Street
London NW1 1DB
a division of Scholastic Ltd
www.scholastic.co.uk
London ~ New York ~ Toronto ~ Sydney ~ Auckland
Mexico City ~ New Delhi ~ Hong Kong

Text copyright © 1995 and 2011 Philip Pullman
Illustrations copyright © 2011 Ian Beck

ISBN 978 1407 12053 9

Aladdin
and the
Enchanted
Lamp

Retold by
Philip Pullman

Illustrated by
Ian Beck

■SCHOLASTIC

Introduction

I have always loved the story of *Aladdin*. It's got everything: comedy, drama, fantasy, magic, fear, excitement, and a terrific plot, as well as a setting that must have been exotic even to the first people who told it; because although it was originally written in an Arabic-speaking part of the world, *Aladdin* itself is set thousands of miles away in China.

Being allowed to tell a great story like this is a privilege and a responsibility as well as a thrill. You have to be true to the shape and the feeling of the original tale, but it's important to add something new as well. If you can't bring something of your own to a story, leave it in the hands of those who can!

It's gone through hundreds of transformations, and been told in dozens of languages. For two centuries at least, it's been one of the best-loved of all pantomimes; it's been told in countless storybooks, and played with in thousands of toy theatres.

There will be many other retellings of *Aladdin* in the future. Telling it in this book was enormous fun, and I am very happy to take my place among those who have passed it on.

Philip Pullman

Once upon a time in China, there lived a boy called Aladdin. He was the son of a tailor called Mustafa, and he made his poor father's life a misery. He ran about the marketplace all day long with a lot of other rogues and scoundrels, getting into trouble, making mischief, and laughing at everyone who tried to make him behave. He wouldn't take up any trade, he wouldn't get a job, and in the end it was too much for Mustafa, who went into a decline and died of worry.

Aladdin's mother was left to look after him on her own. The only work she could find was spinning cotton, so she had to do that while Aladdin hung about the streets with his idle friends.

"Why don't you find some decent work to do, you lazy wretch?" she said.

"Everyone to their trade, mother! You spin cotton and I make mischief. That's a fine trade; it suits me well."

She felt like following her husband to the grave.

One day in the bazaar, as Aladdin was sitting by the fountain flicking water at the passers-by, a certain Moor happened to be sipping mint tea in a nearby coffee shop, twisting his beard into a point and listening to everything that went on. As he heard the name "Aladdin", his ears pricked up, his sharp eyes glittered, and his long fingers curled like claws, because he knew something about Aladdin that Aladdin didn't know.

He watched the boy for some time, and finally he came up to him and said, "Young man, what is your name?"

"Aladdin."

"Not Aladdin the son of Mustafa the tailor?"

"Yes, that's me. But my father's been dead for a year now; there's just me and my mother left."

At that, the Moor began to wail as if his heart was broken. He tore his hair, he pulled his beard, he beat his breast, and the tears ran down his cheeks like rivers down a mountainside. Aladdin was astonished.

"My brother!" the Moor sobbed. "My poor brother Mustafa! I came all this way only to find him dead! Oh, oh, oh, the pity of it – the sorrow of it – but his son is alive, at least! Aladdin, my nephew, heart of my brother's heart, my blood calls out to you!"

And he threw his arms around Aladdin and kissed him on both cheeks. Aladdin was deeply impressed, and so were all his idle friends watching from the fountain nearby, because the Moor was a rich man: he had a silver buckle on his belt and a golden dagger at his waist, and a blood-red ruby sparkled in his turban.

Then Aladdin was even more impressed, because the Moor took out a purse and gave him ten dinars, saying, "Take these to your mother, Aladdin, my dear nephew, and tell her to buy the best food she can find and prepare a meal, and I'll call round tonight and pay my respects to my dear brother's widow. Oh! Oh! Brother of mine! Dead! My heart is broken! Where did you say you lived, dear boy?"

Aladdin realised that the Moor's emotions were so stirred that he'd forgotten his brother's address.

"In the Street of the Oil-Sellers," he said. "Over the house of Shaheed the Nervous Poet."

And off he ran to tell his mother of their good luck. Naturally, she didn't believe a word of it.

"Your poor father never had a brother, you impudent boy! What do you mean by this crazy story? Surely *I'd* know if he had a brother! Get out of the house and find a job! You'll break my heart with your lies and deceptions!"

But he showed her the money and she had to believe *that.* So she went out and bought lamb and rice, and saffron and turmeric, and aubergines and plums and pomegranates, and prepared the best meal she knew how to, just in case.

And sure enough, when the meal was cooked there came a knock on the door, and there was the Moor. He'd changed his robe, and oiled his beard with spikenard, and put a gold pin in his turban, and he looked more gaudy and splendid than ever.

"Oh! My dear brother's wife! My heart is breaking! Oh, these beloved old rooms – the carpet where he and I knelt to pray side by side – the old copper bowl in which he washed his hands – oh, oh, oh!"

And he flung himself to the floor and rolled from side to side, beating his breast with grief. Aladdin was so moved that he began to cry too, but his mother was still a bit suspicious, for the wife of Shaheed the Nervous Poet had given her that copper bowl only the year before. And something else made her uneasy: every single one of the teeth in the Moor's mouth was pointed like a needle.

However, tears are tears, and the man was weeping and wailing so much that Aladdin's mother thought he'd die as well, so she raised him up and said, "Peace be with you, sir, and will you sit and eat the meal I've prepared?"

So they sat down to break bread. As they ate, the Moor told them about his life, and a pack of shameless lies it was too, but Aladdin believed every word of it.

"I spent many years trading in spices between China and Morocco, and I made a great fortune, intending one day to leave it to my dear brother and his family.

"Then I became interested in the learning of the dervishes, the holy men whose wisdom shines brighter than any other. I spent thirty years in the desert with these good and devout men, and then I woke up one day and thought of my brother Mustafa and of his family whom I'd never seen. And at once a great longing to see him filled my heart, and I left that very day, pausing only to say my prayers, and set out on the long journey. Only to find – alas! alas! – my dear brother dead, but a fine son taking his place and looking after his mother as a son should do. How happy that makes me!"

Aladdin looked down and twiddled his thumbs. But his mother said: "I wish Aladdin *was* as good as his father was, sir. I wish he was as good as you.

But in fact he's a scapegrace and a wastrel, and the only money that comes into this house is the little I earn by spinning cotton. And as soon as I get any money the wretch makes off with it. He won't learn a trade, he won't do a steady job, and altogether it broke his father's heart, the way he carried on."

Aladdin felt ashamed. The Moor frowned severely and said, "Oh, dear me, I'm not pleased to hear that. Aladdin, you're nearly a grown man, it's time you started bearing your share of responsibility. But never mind, I'm sure you mean well, and it's just that you haven't found the right opening. Tomorrow morning we'll go and see about setting you up as a merchant with a fine shop of your own."

Aladdin perked up at once, and that night he could hardly sleep for thinking of the splendid clothes he'd wear, and the lordly way he'd order his slaves about, and the rare and choice goods he'd display to his wealthy customers… What should he sell? Carpets, sweetmeats, gold and silver? His dreams were glorious.

Next morning the Moor called early and took Aladdin to the baths, where they washed and perfumed themselves, and then they went to the tailor's, where the Moor paid for a suit of clothes for Aladdin – the finest he'd ever seen.

After that they went to the bazaar, where all the rich merchants gathered to sip coffee and exchange their news, and the Moor joined in, talking of prices and qualities with such an air of knowledge that the other merchants took him for an important man, and bought him spice-cakes and flattered him. Aladdin was included in all his lordly talk, and he felt no end of a fine fellow.

When they left the bazaar, the Moor said, "Now, I've got something very special to show you, Aladdin. Come with me and you'll see a garden full of wonders, something no-one else has ever seen."

The Moor could do nothing wrong now as far as Aladdin was concerned. If he wanted to look at gardens full of wonders Aladdin was only too happy to go along.

"Where is the garden, Uncle?"

"Up in the mountains, my boy. No-one knows of it

but me. Step out, now. We've got a long walk ahead of us."

The Moor's long legs set off like scissors, and Aladdin had to trot fast to keep up with him.

After many hours they were so high up in the mountains that they could no longer see the city. Finally the moor stopped, and looked around carefully, and measured the distance from a certain rock to a bush close by, and stepped out four paces beyond that.

Aladdin watched, mystified. This was no garden; it was a hideous, barren place with nothing but sand and dry bushes and lizards.

"Uncle, where is the garden?" he said. "I can see nothing but—"

Thwack!

The Moor fetched Aladdin such a crack round the head that he thought his brains would run out of his ears.

"Ow! What was that for? Not even my father hit me that hard! Ow!"

"That was to teach you a lesson," said the Moor, smiling sharply. "The magic I'm going to perform is extremely dangerous. Watch, say nothing, and learn."

The Moor gathered some sticks, struck a light with

his tinderbox, and blew it into a flame. When it was burning brightly he took a handful of powder from a pouch at his belt and sprinkled it on the fire.

At once there was a puff of green smoke and a modest clap of thunder, and when the smoke had cleared there was a large flat stone set in the ground where the fire had been.

"There," said the Moor proudly. "Lift the stone, Aladdin."

"What? By myself?"

"Aha! Just read what it says."

Aladdin bent down, and saw, carved into the ancient stone, the words:

THIS STONE CAN BE LIFTED ONLY BY ALADDIN, THE SON OF MUSTAFA.

"Well!" said Aladdin. "Well, that's amazing!"

He took hold of the ring in the stone, and up it came as if it were made of paper.

"Now listen carefully," said the Moor. "Go down these narrow steps and you'll find yourself in a passage with a door at the end. Open it and go through, and you'll be in a beautiful garden with trees bearing all

kinds of fruit. Whatever you do, don't touch them, or you'll certainly be turned at once into a black stone, d'you understand? Go through this garden to a terrace at the end, where you'll see a lamp hanging from a chain. Take down the lamp and empty the oil out of it, and bring it back to me. On the way back you can pick the fruit, if you like. Now, in you go. Once I have... Once *we* have that lamp, the world is ours!"

Aladdin couldn't wait. He dived into the hole like a terrier. It was narrow and dark, and stuffy and dusty, and he banged his head and scraped his elbows, but he was too excited to mind that. When he got to the bottom, he felt his way along the passage, and it was just as the Moor had said: there was a door at the end. Aladdin felt for the handle and turned it.

The Moor had told him what to expect, but when he opened the door he could hardly breathe for astonishment. He took a little shaky step and held on to the door-frame, looking all around with eyes as wide open as his mouth.

There under the ground was a beautiful garden spreading out on all sides, lit by red, white and pink blossoms on the oleander trees, on each petal of which sat a family of fireflies, sipping nectar and glowing like lanterns. There were tall cypresses and wide-spreading cedar trees, there were vines and roses and pergolas trailing with sweet-scented jasmine, there were fountains and streams and gazebos, and a nightingale sang in the dark night air.

Aladdin and the Enchanted Lamp

Mindful of what the Moor had said, Aladdin didn't touch a thing, but walked wonderingly along the path to the marble terrace at the end where, sure enough, there hung a lamp.

Aladdin blew it out, emptied the oil from it, and was about to leave when he thought, "It's a shame to go straight back without looking around. I might never have another chance, after all."

So he looked along the terrace and saw all manner of strange things. Here there was a cage containing a salamander wreathed in flames, with a notice underneath it in a language Aladdin couldn't read. Next there was a glass bottle in which an imp was prisoned, who beat the glass with his tiny fists and snarled with rage as Aladdin laughed; there was a notice in a different language under this one. Then there was a snake swallowing its tail, and as its mouth moved along the tail its neck grew behind it, so it stayed the same size; and there was a butterfly with a human face tethered by a golden chain no thicker than a hair, and dozens of other wonders, and by each of them was a notice in a different language: in Persian, in Turkish, in Greek, even in outlandish tongues like English.

Finally he came to one he could read. It said, *Whoever wears me will be safe from any harm,* and the object it referred to was a plain ring of dull, black iron.

"It must be for me!" he thought. "They wrote it so I could read it, after all."

It was too tempting to leave. Aladdin slipped the ring on his finger, and just at that moment he heard the Moor shouting:

"Aladdin! Aladdin!"

His voice was magnified by the tunnel, and he sounded like an evil spirit calling. Aladdin tucked the lamp into his clothes and ran back through the garden, snatching at the glittering fruits on the trees as he passed and thrusting them into his pockets.

When he reached the tunnel, the Moor was screaming with anger, gnashing his teeth and clenching his fists, but as soon as he saw Aladdin his expression changed and he smiled sweetly.

"There you are, dear boy! I was so worried, I thought you'd turned into a black stone! Have you got the lamp?"

"Yes, Uncle."

"Hand it up, then, hand it up!"

"Help me out first, Uncle, then I'll give you the lamp."

"Curse you! Do as I say! The lamp, boy, the lamp!"

Well, Aladdin was no fool. He'd begun to suspect the Moor as soon as he got that clout on the head, and the way he was carrying on now gave him away completely.

"You're no uncle!" Aladdin cried. "You're a sorcerer!"

With a scream louder than any before, the Moor stamped his foot and threw some powder in the air, and at once the earth groaned and shook and the entrance to the tunnel closed up. So did the door to the garden of wonders, and there was poor Aladdin, trapped beneath the earth.

He beat and beat at the stone above him, shouting and shouting to be let out. The darkness got right into his eyes, and the earth absorbed his shouts like water: they sank in at once and vanished. Sobbing with fear, he felt his way down the steps to the door of the garden, but it was gone; the passage was blind, and the darkness was terrible. Not the faintest flicker of light shone there, not even the ghost of a glow-worm glimmered. He was buried alive.

Of course, Aladdin had been right about the Moor. He was no relation at all, but a dervish, a learned man, and cunning with it: he knew all there was to know about astrology and palmistry and sand-magic and water-magic and fire-magic. His mystic powers had shown him that there was a fabulous treasure under the Chinese city of Al-Kolo-Ats, which could only be retrieved by a youth called Aladdin, so he had sought first the city and then the youth, with the results we've seen. If only he'd been a little more patient, he would have had the lamp in his hands. As it was, he had nothing, so he stamped and roared with fury and disappointment, and went back home to nurse his vengeance. But so much for him.

Aladdin and the Enchanted Lamp

Aladdin spent three days beneath the earth. He tried to dig himself out, but wherever he put his hands they met hard rough rock, and no matter how desperately he scraped or how painfully he tore his fingernails, he couldn't dislodge a fragment.

He fell asleep with tears in his eyes, and when he awoke the tears were still there, and nothing had changed. He prayed, he cried for his mother, he cursed the Moor with all the curses he knew and several he invented, and it made no difference. Then he felt hungry, and remembered the fruit he'd snatched from the trees in the magic garden, but it was a mockery: his pockets were full of stones. He was too full of despair even to throw them away. After three days of this hideous torment he was ready to die, and he fell to the ground and wrung his hands in anguish; and as he did so, he happened to rub the iron ring he'd picked up from the terrace. He'd completely forgotten about it.

At once there was a clap of thunder, and a space cleared in the darkness. He could see it, though it was still dark, and there was a figure there: black skin, black beard, black robes, but eyes like windows into a fire.

Aladdin saw it by the light from those eyes, reflected dimly from the rock all around; and the figure was bowing to him.

"I am here, Master!" said the apparition.

"Who are you?"

"I am the Jinnee of the Ring, your bounden slave. You have summoned me. I have come. How can I help you?"

Aladdin was so astonished he could hardly breathe, but he gathered his wits and said, "In that case, I order you to take me back to the surface of the earth."

The Jinnee bowed and vanished. Immediately, the earth rumbled and groaned, and Aladdin felt himself being rushed upwards. A moment later he was standing in the open air, blinking and rubbing his eyes at the brightness of the light. When he could see, he recognised the place by the ashes of the fire the Moor had lit three days before.

Blessing his good luck, he set off for the city at once, tired and dirty and hungry as he was. He stumbled into the Street of the Oil-Sellers and up the stairs beside the house of Shaheed the Nervous Poet, and his mother greeted him with sobs of joy.

"Mother!" he cried, embracing her. "I've had a miraculous escape! That wretch of a Moor tried to kill me, but a powerful jinnee brought me out of the ground safely – oh, I'm hungry! Oh, I'm worn out!"

His mother hurried to make a meal with the only food she had in the house. As they ate, he told her everything that had happened.

"Well, I never did trust him," she said. "I saw through him, don't you worry. But go and lie down, dear, I've made your bed."

Aladdin slept for a whole day and night. When he woke up, she could tell his experience hadn't changed him, because the first thing he did was to call, "Mother! I'm hungry! Get me something to eat!"

The poor woman said, "We've got nothing to eat in the house, dear. Let me spin a bit of cotton and I'll go and sell it to buy food."

Then Aladdin clapped his hands and said, "What am I thinking of? We can sell the lamp I brought up from the garden of wonders!"

He took it out of his pocket and showed her.

"Well, it's not very clean, is it?" she said doubtfully. "Let me give it a bit of a polish first."

So she began to rub it with a cloth, and as soon as she did so there was a phenomenal clap of thunder. She dropped the lamp at once and clung to Aladdin, and he clung to her, because they both thought the house was going to fall down.

But then he pointed. "Look, Mother! The lamp!"

For out of the spout of the lamp, a twist of smoke with two sparks in it was rapidly twirling upwards, and the sound of a rushing wind filled the little room. In less than a second, the smoke rose to the ceiling and turned black and solid, bulging and glistening and shining like smooth dark flesh, and the two sparks flared into flame, settled down in their sockets, and became eyes. And then it wasn't smoke at all, nor human flesh: it was a mighty jinnee. He could have reached out his great hand and pinched Aladdin to death as easily as you could pinch a mosquito.

Aladdin's mother was clinging to him, trembling. She whispered, "It's your jinnee, Aladdin! Make him go away!"

Aladdin said, "This isn't the Jinnee of the Ring! That one was a different shape. Who are you, Jinnee?"

"I am the Jinnee of the Lamp!" said the great spirit, in a voice that shook the rafters. "Whatever you command me, I will obey, I and the other slaves of the lamp."

"In that case, I command you to go and bring us some food at once."

"At once, great master," said the Jinnee courteously, and disappeared with a faint but powerful whooshing noise.

Aladdin's mother was weak with astonishment. She looked at her son with new eyes. There she'd been, thinking Aladdin was an idle good-for-nothing, and all the time he could command jinnees without turning a hair.

After a moment or two, the Jinnee came back and clapped his enormous hands. Up the stairs in through the door of Aladdin's house there came a procession of slaves. Each slave carried a plate or a dish or a bowl of gold or silver, and in each dish there was some delicious-smelling food, with the steam still rising from the hot dishes and a frost of condensation on the ice creams and the fruit sherbets.

"Here we are, Mother! All the food we can eat!" cried Aladdin.

When the slaves had set it down, they all bowed and trooped towards the lamp, getting smaller and smaller as they did so, and one after another they popped into the spout and disappeared. The last to go was the Jinnee, who turned himself back into a column of smoke before twisting himself neatly into the same hole.

"Eat, Mother!" said Aladdin.

They lived on that food for three days, and it was the best food they'd ever had.

When it had gone, Aladdin decided to carry one of the gold plates to the market to sell, because he'd been quite taken with the idea of becoming a merchant, and thought he'd still try his skill.

The first goldsmith he went to could hardly believe his luck. He'd never seen such a fine piece of gold. He stuck out his lower lip and tried to look doubtful.

"Well... I don't know... This style's not very fashionable any more... Tell you what, I'll give you two dinars, as a favour."

Aladdin, who had no idea what the plate was worth, took the money happily and bought some food. When that food ran out he did the same thing again, and each time he took the goldsmith a plate, he only got two dinars for it.

When half the plates were sold, he took the next one to the market as usual, but this time he was stopped by an honest goldsmith who'd seen him pass each day and wondered what he had for sale.

"But this is wonderful!" he exclaimed when he saw the plate. "And is this like all the others?"

"More or less. Some of the others were bigger."

"And how much did he give you for them?"

"Two dinars each," said Aladdin. "Are they worth more, then?"

"This dish is worth no less than eighty dinars! In fact, I'll give you that for it here and now. That man's been cheating you, my boy!"

So Aladdin saw that there were other rogues in the world as well as the Moor. He took the rest of the plates to the honest goldsmith, who paid him a fair price, and so Aladdin and his mother began to gain a fortune. The honest goldsmith did more than that, though. He told Aladdin a great deal about buying and selling, about the prices and qualities of merchandise. He told Aladdin something else as well: the stones he had brought away from the garden of wonders, the ones he had plucked from the trees thinking they were fruit, were none other than jewels of fabulous value, which only needed cutting and polishing to be seen in all their beauty.

So Aladdin left his old life altogether, and didn't seek out the company of spongers and loafers as he'd used to. Instead he spent hours talking to jewellers and goldsmiths and other merchants, learning how to judge the quality of goods, and he soon came to realise that none of the jewels they sold could compare with even the smallest of those from the garden of wonders, and which he'd tried to eat in desperation when he was imprisoned under the ground. So Aladdin grew both in wisdom and in wealth.

One day Aladdin was in the market when a herald came by shouting: "Make way! Make way for the Princess Badr-al-Budur, the daughter of his Most Exulted Sublimity the Sultan of China! Everyone is to close their shops, their doors, their windows and their eyes until she has passed on her way to the Baths, by the Sultan's orders!"

Aladdin and the Enchanted Lamp

Aladdin was immensely curious to see the Princess. He ran to the Baths and hid among the branches of a fig tree outside the doors, and as Princess Badr-al-Budur came near, followed by her female slaves, she lifted her veil for a moment before entering, and Aladdin saw her face.

He felt as if lightning had struck his heart. He couldn't breathe, his head was spinning, he nearly fell out of the fig tree. When he'd recovered a little, he staggered home and said, "Mother! Make my bed! I'm not well… Something has happened to me… I saw the Princess Badr-al-Budur and now I don't know if I'm in paradise or in hell. Only yesterday, I thought all women looked like you under their veils, Mother, all wrinkled and ugly! But now I'll have no rest, I'll die, I'll never have a moment's peace until I marry her."

His mother threw up her hands.

"My dear son, you must have lost your wits along with your heart. What makes you think the Sultan would ever take you for a son-in-law? Put it out of your mind! There are plenty of girls, and they don't all look like me, whatever it was you said, all wrinkly and so on. Besides, you need someone to call on the Sultan and ask for her hand. You mustn't do that yourself.

But who would go for you?"

"Why, you, of course, Mother! But look, it won't be so hard after all. When the Sultan sees my jewels he won't be able to resist."

And he took a fine dish and arranged on it the jewels from the garden of wonders. They shone and sparkled with such lustre and beauty that even Aladdin's mother was convinced, and she hastened away to the palace.

It was the Sultan's custom to listen to the pleas of any of his subjects who wanted to see him, and Aladdin's mother reached the palace to find the Throne Room packed. As well as the Grand Vizier and the ten Petty Viziers, the Nabobs and the Emirs and the Pashas, the Janissaries and the Bashi-Bazouks, the Barmecides, the Bimbashis and the Beys, there were poor people by the dozens, all with things to beg of the Sultan. Aladdin's mother stood humbly at the edge of the room with the plate of jewels covered by her second-best tablecloth, and waited while the Sultan attended to his petitioners.

He judged all the cases, granted some requests, ordered some punishments, and dealt with everything fairly and wisely until only Aladdin's mother was left.

"Leave her till tomorrow, Sire," said the Grand Vizier.

"She's only a poor old woman, she doesn't matter."

"No, she's come to see me, so I'll listen to her," said the Sultan. "What did you want, old lady?"

Aladdin's mother trembled all over.

"I hope Your Majesty will forgive me this request," she said, in such a tiny voice they could hardly hear it.

"Speak up!" said the Grand Vizier.

"Yes, sir, yes, sir, I've come on behalf of my dear son Aladdin, Your Sublimity. The fact is that he accidentally caught a glimpse of the lovely Princess Badr-al-Budur yesterday, and he fell in love, and he's asked me to come and beg for her hand."

As she said that, the poor woman's voice gave out altogether.

"Your Majesty," the Vizier said haughtily, "the wretch ought to be flogged by the Master of the Torments until his ribs lie bare! To have gazed unlawfully upon the beauty of the Princess deserves a thousand lashes at least. Besides," he went on more quietly, so that only the Sultan could hear, "Your Majesty will forgive me for reminding you that I had hoped for the Princess's hand for my son Mahboob."

The Sultan took no notice, because he was interested in the bundle that Aladdin's mother was carrying.

"What's that in the bundle, madam?" he said. "You're clinging to it as if it were full of jewels."

For answer, Aladdin's mother set the dish at the foot of the throne and humbly removed the second-best tablecloth. The glitter of the jewels lit up the Throne Room like a thousand torches, and the Grand Vizier had to blink and shade his eyes.

"Well, what do you say to that, Grand Vizier?" said the Sultan. "Have *I* got any jewels like those?"

"Not one," said the Grand Vizier, grinding his teeth.

"No. And if he's got presents like *that* to give me… Well, I don't know what to say. What do you suggest?"

The Grand Vizier made an irritable gesture with his hand, as if he were dismissing a beggar.

"Ask for forty slaves," he said, "each carrying a dish of pure gold, each dish to be filled with jewels like those. He'll never be able to manage that."

"Good idea," said the Sultan. "Madam! Tell your son Aladdin that I'll be glad to let my daughter marry him as long as he brings me… What was it?"

The Grand Vizier went through it again, and Aladdin's mother nodded.

"Thank you very much, Your Majesty, " she said, curtseying deeply. "My son will be overjoyed, I'll go and tell him at once."

And she left happily. She thought that Aladdin would never be able to get all that treasure together, but at least he wouldn't be sent to the Master of the Torments, so he'd get away scot-free if only he put that silly idea of marrying the Princess out of his mind.

But when she told him what the Sultan had said, he clapped his hands and jumped for joy.

"Nothing easier!" he said. "Where's the lamp?"

He rubbed the lamp and the Jinnee appeared at once, just as before. This time Aladdin was prepared for it, but he still felt a little nervous as the monstrous

Jinnee materialised out of the smoke. His mother covered her eyes.

"As you command, so I shall obey," said the Jinnee. "What is your wish, Master?"

"I want forty slaves, each carrying a dish of gold *that* big – no, make it twice as big: *this* big – and each dish is to be full of jewels like the one I sent to the Sultan today. Or even better."

"At once, Master," said the Jinnee, and began to turn himself into smoke again. In the morning there was a knock at the door, and forty slave-girls in shimmering silken veils, each one very nearly as beautiful as

Aladdin and the Enchanted Lamp

Princess Badr-al-Budur herself, came crowding up the narrow stairs. Each slave-girl was carrying a golden dish big enough to hold a turkey, and each dish was brim-full of rubies and emeralds, of diamonds and sapphires, of pearls and opals and amethysts. The smallest of the jewels was as large as Aladdin's big toe, and the largest was bigger than his fist. As the slave-girls climbed the stairs, Shaheed the Nervous Poet peeped around the edge of his door in wonder; he thought he was imagining it all. Soon Aladdin's little room was full, and the floor was creaking.

Once he'd counted them to make sure there were forty, Aladdin sent them downstairs to line up. Then, at the head of the procession, he set off through the streets towards the palace. Naturally, they attracted a big crowd, and soon hundreds of people were following to see what was going to happen.

In the Throne Room, the Sultan and the Grand Vizier and the ten Petty Viziers, the Nabobs and the Emirs and the Pashas, the Janissaries and the Bashi-Bazouks, the Barmecides, the Bimbashis and the Beys all fell silent as they heard the clamour outside.

Then the Eunuch of the Doorway flung open the door and announced: "Your Majesty! Aladdin and his forty slaves, with their presents for Your Amplitude!"

And in came the slave-girls, to the accompaniment of invisible gongs and flutes and soft cymbals. The Grand Vizier counted. After the slaves had laid their golden dishes at the Sultan's feet, Aladdin himself strode in, looking every inch a prince worthy of all this wealth.

"Greetings, Mighty Sultan!" he said proudly. "I bring you these grains of dull sand which are not fit to be scattered under your feet, in the hope that you will excuse their inadequacy as a dowry for the hand of the incomparable Princess Badr-al-Budur."

The Sultan blinked and puffed out his cheeks and leant forward to plunge his hands into the nearest dish. As he let the jewels fall through his fingers, the light splintered into a thousand rainbows.

"Well!" said the Sultan. "You've brought us what we asked for, Aladdin. I never saw such wondrous jewels. Did you, Grand Vizier?"

"No," snarled the Grand Vizier.

"Haven't got much choice, have we? We did promise."

"But what do we know of his background, Sire? And jewels are all very well, but where is he going to take the Princess to live?"

The Sultan nodded sagely.

"Where do you live, Aladdin?" he said.

"In the Street of the Oil-Sellers, Your Majesty, over the house of Shaheed the Nervous Poet. But," he added quickly, "I don't expect the Princess to come and live there. I shall build her a palace, naturally."

"Aha!" said the Grand Vizier. "You'll never be able to do *that.*"

"Oh, yes, he will," said all the slave-girls.

"Oh, no, he won't. Tell him, Your Majesty,

you require a splendid palace built for Princess Badr-al-Budur on that patch of empty ground beyond the fountain."

"H'mm," said the Sultan. "All right, Aladdin, one more little thing. Build a palace for Badr-al-Budur, and then she's yours, my boy."

"With pleasure, Mighty Sultan, and I'll have it done by the morning. Good day to you!"

And with a deep bow he left the Throne Room, and the Grand Vizier and the ten Petty Viziers, the Nabobs and the Emirs and the Pashas, the Janissaries and the Bashi-Bazouks, the Barmecides, the Bimbashis and the Beys all bowed back automatically, because he looked like a prince already.

Back at home, he rubbed the lamp again.

"Yes, O Master?"

"I want a palace built on the patch of ground behind the Sultan's fountain. I want a dome of gold, and pillars of lapis lazuli and onyx, and a floor of marble; I want gardens and fountains and courtyards planted with jasmine and roses; I want a retine of slaves and cooks and major-domos and eunuchs and so on.

Each window must be made of a single enormous diamond, and in some fountains I want wine flowing, in some water, and I want one to spray perfume to scent the air; and I want the finest, softest carpets from Shiraz and Bokhara; and I want harps and lutes hanging in every room, so that when a breeze blows, music plays by itself. Now, as for the Princess's bedroom…"

He described the whole palace to the Jinnee, who stood shimmering silently in front of him. When he'd finished, he added: "Oh, and I mustn't forget – it's to be done by tomorrow morning, please."

"Nothing could be easier, Master."

Aladdin went to bed happily. When he woke up, he summoned the Jinnee once again.

"All done?"

"I endeavour to give satisfaction, Master. All is complete."

"I don't know how you do it, Jinnee. Have a horse at the door in ten minutes. Better have a retinue of slaves as well. And a nice dress for my mother, and some slave-girls to attend her. And one of those chair things to carry her in."

"Very good, Master."

So when Aladdin rode up to the Sultan's palace at the head of his slaves, no-one in the court had seen such splendour. And the Princess Badr-al-Budur herself, watching from an upstairs window, saw Aladdin curvetting and leaping on his glossy black horse and fell in love with him at once.

And that very day they were married. But so much for them.

When the Moor got back to Morocco after leaving Aladdin buried alive, he beat his slaves and cursed and raved and stormed with fury. His only consolation was that Aladdin was certainly dead, and would never be able to use the lamp and command its wonders.

But as time went by, the Moor began to feel his heart gnawing at his ribs with desire for the lamp again. How could he get it? He did some sand-magic to find out exactly where it was, by throwing a handful of sand on the floor and looking up the shapes in a book. Rage! Abominable curses! Not only was Aladdin alive, but he'd discovered the use of the lamp, and he was married to a princess, and he had become the master of uncountable riches!

The Moor gnashed his teeth so violently that sparks flew out of his mouth. Then he saddled a camel and set off at once for China, thinking all the way about how he could trick Aladdin out of the lamp.

When he arrived, he'd thought of a good plan. He went to a coppersmith and said, "Make me a dozen lamps, as quick as you can. No, I'm not going to haggle, charge me what you like."

Then he went off to hang about the streets and listen to the gossip. Everywhere he went, he heard praises of Aladdin and the Princess.

"He's so generous!"

"He's as handsome as he is rich!"

"What a lovely couple they make!"

"And have you *seen* the palace he's built her? There's a cage in every room, containing an invisible spirit who plays music whenever he snaps his fingers!"

"And even his slaves eat off gold plates…"

The Moor listened, with savage envy chewing his innards. But there was a hot and hopeful glee bubbling there as well, as he thought that all that wealth would soon be his.

When the copper lamps were ready, bright and new and gleaming, the Moor hung them around his neck and took them to the market.

"New lamps for old! New lamps for old!" he cried.

The passers-by could hardly believe their ears.

"New lamps? For *old*? You mean if I bring you a dirty old lamp —"

"I'll give you a shiny new one in exchange, yes, that's right."

"But why?"

"To fulfil a vow I made at the shrine of Omar the Caliph," said the Moor piously.

"Right! Good! I'll have one!"

And within a few minutes, the first ten lamps were gone.

Aladdin had gone hunting for the day, and the Princess Badr-al-Budur was at a palace window, where she liked to sit and watch what was going on. She heard all the commotion and called her favourite slave, Fatima.

"What's happening in the marketplace, Fatima?"

"There's a Moor, Your Highness, and he's giving new lamps away for old ones. He's probably crazy. All the urchins and ragamuffins are laughing at him."

"I'd like to see if he really means it," said the Princess. "But we haven't got any old lamps. What a shame! Everything's new here."

"The Master's got an old lamp in his apartments, Your Highness. I was going to polish it for him and he said to leave it alone, not to touch it, it wasn't worth bothering with."

"Oh, good! Go and get it, Fatima. He'll be pleased we've got a new one in exchange."

So Fatima took the enchanted lamp to the Moor, who recognised it at once. His eyes sharpened, his lips drew back from his teeth, and all his hair prickled under his turban.

"Here you are," he said, giving her his last new one, "and I hope it shines brightly for your master, ha ha. This is the one I want!"

And he threw the other lamps down in a heap and ran off to find a quiet spot. All the urchins and ragamuffins grabbed at the old lamps and sold them at once, but they didn't get much for them.

After a minute or so, the Moor found a dusty little patch of ground between the municipal slaughterhouse and the public baths, where he held up the lamp and kissed it and fondled it and stroked it, moaning with delight. Then he gave it good hard rub.

The Jinnee appeared at once.

"Yes, O Master? Whatever you command I shall obey, for I am the slave of him who holds the lamp. What is your wish?"

The Moor was gloating so much he could scarcely think.

"My wish – what do I wish? Aha! Yes! I want you to lift up Aladdin's palace, with everything in it, and take it all the way to Morocco. Put it down in my garden."

"At once, O Master!"

The Jinnee twirled himself round and round, getting bigger and bigger, and then he reached down and lifted the palace as if it were a bowl of nuts. Then he whisked it away and dwindled to a spot in the sky in less than three seconds.

"And then come back for me!" shouted the Moor.

Ten seconds later the Jinnee did, and thus the Moor escaped with his prize.

When Aladdin came back from hunting, he found the Grand Vizier waiting at the gates of the city, at the head of a troop of Janissaries armed with scimitars.

"Arrest him!" the Vizier commanded, and before Aladdin could say a word, he was pinioned in chains and brought before the Sultan.

"Well, impudent youth?" roared the Sultan, who was trembling with rage. "Where is my daughter?"

"In our palace, good king, where I left her this morning."

"And where's the palace?"

Aladdin was too astonished to answer.

"I told you, Your Majesty!" the Grand Vizier crowed. "I said he wasn't to be trusted! Send for the Master of the Torments!"

"Your Majesty," said Aladdin, "some horrible magic is at work. I beg you to give me just one day and if I haven't found both the Princess and the palace, you can cut my head off. That's a promise."

He looked so brave and honest that the Sultan found himself saying, "Oh, well, all right. Twenty-four hours then."

So they set Aladdin free. He went to look at the hole where his palace had been, and he knew at once that only the Moor could have played such a trick.

As he stood there scratching his head, Fatima the slave-girl saw him and came running up in dismay.

"Master! The lamp! The Moor! The palace! The Princess! Oh, forgive me!"

And she told him everything. Aladdin was in despair. He cried out aloud and wrung his hands, and in doing so, he accidentally rubbed the iron ring, which he had never taken off.

The ground shook, and a space cleared itself in the air, and there stood the Jinnee of the Ring. This time he was the same colour as daylight, so it was hard to see him, but his eyes glowed like windows in a burning house.

"Yes, O Master?"

"Do you know the Jinnee of the Lamp?"

"Indeed, Great One."

"Well, he was my slave! Why has he taken my palace away?"

"Forgive me, Lord, but he is not your slave, he is the slave of whoever holds the lamp. And what is more, his power is far greater than mine."

"Do you know where he has taken the palace?"

"To Morocco, Master."

"And could you take me and Fatima there?"

"*Me*?" said Fatima.

"As soon as you wish, Master."

"Then do so now."

"But what —" Fatima began.

The Jinnee of the Ring lifted Aladdin and Fatima into the sky and whooshed them away at very nearly the speed of light.

They flew over India and Persia, over Baghdad and Jerusalem and the Mosque of Omar and over Cairo and the Pyramids, over the great desert and the Atlas Mountains.

Then the Jinnee put them down in the Moor's garden in the shade of a tamarind tree.

"— do you want *me* to do?" finished Fatima, breathless.

"The Moor is holding Princess Badr-al-Budur prisoner," explained Aladdin. "And I want to finish the rascal off for good."

He looked around the Moor's garden, and saw at once what he needed. Beneath the fever-trees, beds of noxious plants were laid out for the Moor to work his venomous magic with. Aladdin picked one leaf each of scorpionflax, dreambane, and herb-of-agony, and gave them to Fatima wrapped in a handkerchief.

"Go into the palace and find your mistress," he said, "and tell her that when the Moor comes to her this evening, she must squeeze the juice of these leaves into his wine and see that he drinks it. They'll make him fall into a deep sleep. Then she must let me in at once."

Fatima went into the palace and found Badr-al-Budur.

"Oh Fatima!" said the Princess. "How glad I am to see you. But how did you get here?"

"Prince Aladdin is here too, Your Highness! He's hiding in the garden. We came here on a jinnee!"

The Princess regained her courage at once.

"Is Aladdin really here? Oh, I'd do anything to get away from that horrible sorcerer! If I had a sword, I'd cut off his hairy head."

"You must take these herbs, Your Highness…"

Fatima told her exactly what to do, and they settled down to wait.

That evening, the Moor came to knock on the door of the Princess's apartments, just as Aladdin had known that he would. Fatima opened the door, and in he came with a big bunch of roses in one hand, a big box of Turkish Delight in the other, and red pointed slippers on his feet. He had perfumed his beard and polished his nails and carefully snipped the hairs out of his nose.

"My luscious little peach!" he said. "My pretty little Bibble-Bubble! I have come to eat with you, and I'll tell you straight away, I mean to be your husband. A sorcerer like me is quite a catch, I can assure you. But let's sit down on these soft and silken cushions, and feast. Slaves! Bring in the food!"

A troop of slaves brought in dishes of roast camel and grilled lamb, of rice and couscous and bread and fruit of every kind, and jars of chilled wine.

Badr-al-Budur pretended she was enjoying it. All through the meal she smiled and teased and flirted with him, and when they'd finished eating, she said: "I'd like to show you a custom of my country, O great one. When lovers want to exchange vows, they drink from each other's cup. Let me drink from yours, O handsome and fragrant sorcerer."

Delighted, the Moor let her sip from his cup. He didn't see her squeeze the herbs into hers. Then she gave him a kiss.

"Such melonious lips!" he cried, intoxicated, and drank her cup down at once, eager for another kiss.

But he never got another kiss in his life. Something ghastly was happening inside him. The herb-juice dried his lungs and squeezed his heart and froze his blood, and he dropped to the floor like a stone.

Badr-al-Budur ran to the window and flung it wide. "Aladdin! Aladdin!"

He jumped in at once, and they kissed each other lovingly, but couldn't kiss for long because there was still work to be done.

Aladdin opened the sorcerer's robe, and there was the lamp. He took it at once, and when he had it safe, he said to Badr-al-Budur: "Leave the room, my dear. I'm going to dispose of this wretch for good and all."

So she went out, and Aladdin took his sword and cut off the Moor's head. That was the end of him, and no mistake.

Then Aladdin rubbed the lamp, and the Jinnee appeared.

"Yes, O Master? I am your slave, I and the other slaves of the lamp."

"Tell me, Jinnee: if the Moor had asked you to kill me, would you have done it?"

"I would have cracked your skull like a flea in less than a moment, Master, for I am the slave of whoever holds the lamp, you or another."

"I see. Did you bring the palace here, Jinnee?"

"Indeed I did, Master."

"And can you take it back again?"

"In the twinkling of an eye, sir."

"Then do so at once."

The Jinnee swirled out through the window, and a moment later Aladdin and Badr-al-Budur and Fatima felt a slight jerk as the foundations were plucked out of the ground. But so smoothly did the Jinnee carry them that they knew nothing about the flight, until five seconds later there was a tiny bump. That was the palace being set down in China again.

The Sultan was overjoyed to see them back. He had been terrified in case anything had happened to Badr-al-Budur, who was his only child, and when he saw the golden palace all bright and glittering in the evening air, his eyes filled with tears of happiness. He ran down the stairs and across the court of fountains and embraced the Princess, who was coming out to meet him. Then he embraced Aladdin too.

"My dear, dear daughter! And my beloved son-in-law! Where did you go? How did you find her? And what's the cause of all this magic?"

So Aladdin explained about the Moor, and the lamp, and how Fatima had exchanged it not knowing the secret, and everything.

"And if you doubt my word, Your Majesty, come and see the wretch's body in the other room," he said.

The Sultan was appalled at the danger they'd been in.

"Take his body away and burn it!" he ordered. "Scatter his ashes to the four winds! I don't want anything left of this horrible enchanter."

So that was done, and then the Sultan ordered a festival. There was a month's feasting and dancing, and flags hung on all the public buildings, and there was free wine for everyone, as much as they wanted.

Aladdin's mother came to live in her own apartments in the palace, and never had to spin cotton again; the honest goldsmith was rewarded, and the bad one punished; and Aladdin paid Shaheed the Nervous Poet a thousand dinars to write the story of the Enchanted Lamp. Blessed be Aladdin, prince of publishers! May every poor writer of stories find a patron as generous and wise!

But as for the lamp itself, Aladdin hid it away and never told anyone where he put it.

So he and Badr-al-Budur were reunited, and they loved each other more than ever. And when at last the Sultan died, Aladdin inherited the kingdom. He ruled justly and well all his long life, until he died, old and wise and surrounded by his many and many children and grandchildren, some of them almost as naughty as he had once been, but all of them brave, and beautiful, and greatly beloved.

The End

Philip Pullman

Born in Norwich in 1946, Philip Pullman is a world-renowned writer. His novels have won every major award for children's fiction, and are now also established as adult bestsellers.

In 2003, the *His Dark Materials* trilogy came third in the BBC's Big Read competition to find the nation's favourite book.

In 2005 he was awarded the Astrid Lindgren Memorial Award, the world's biggest prize for children's literature.

Philip is married with two grown-up children, and lives in Oxford.

Ian Beck

Ian Beck is a well-loved, award-winning author and illustrator. Born in 1947, he worked as a freelance artist for many years, creating artwork for magazines and album covers – including the iconic image that appears on Elton John's *Goodbye Yellow Brick Road*.

He began working on children's books in 1982 and has since published more than sixty picture books. He is also the author of a number of novels for children and young adults including the *Tom Trueheart* series.

Ian and Philip have collaborated on a number of projects including an anniversary edition of the *His Dark Materials* trilogy.

Ian is married and has three children.

Aladdin and the Enchanted Lamp